The Ghost Family Meets Its Match

story and pictures by Nicole Rubel

Dial Books for Young Readers New York

Published by Dial Books for Young Readers
A Division of Penguin Books USA Inc.
375 Hudson Street
New York, New York 10014

Copyright © 1992 by Nicole Rubel
All rights reserved
Designed by Amelia Lau Carling
Printed in the U.S.A.
First Edition
1 3 5 7 9 10 8 6 4 2

Library of Congress Cataloging in Publication Data
Rubel, Nicole.
The Ghost family meets its match / by Nicole Rubel. — 1st ed.
p.   cm.
Summary: For a century, a family of ghosts successfully scares
everyone away from their haunted house, until some new tenants move
in with a surprise of their own.
ISBN 0-8037-1093-3 (trade).   ISBN 0-8037-1094-1 (library)
[1. Ghosts—Fiction.] I. Title.
PZ7.R828Gh 1992 [E]—dc20 91-10815 CIP AC

The art for this book was prepared with black ink
and colored markers. The artwork was then color-separated
and reproduced in full color.

To Janet, Atha, and Amelia

Thank you.

During the 1880s a large house was built by a famous explorer.
One day the explorer went on an African journey. He sent back
many souvenirs of his trip, but he never came home himself. The
house was empty for years, until a family of ghosts flew in.

"Perfect!" said Father Ghost. "This house is really gruesome!"
"Dust and cobwebs everywhere," said Mother Ghost. "I love it!"

"The attic will be great for the bats," said their son Igor.
"Creepy Cat is purring," said their daughter Ivy.
So the Ghosts stayed and haunted their new house very happily.

Two years later a horse-and-carriage rumbled up the path to the house.

"Look," said Horace Blake. "Here's a house that's big enough for our family."

"Indeed!" said Amelia Blake.

They stopped the horse and got out. But when they got to the
front door, they heard someone howling BOOOOO! and they turned
right around.

The Blakes left in haste.

During the 1920s Todd and Violet Wagner were on their way
to a tea party.
"My goodness," Todd said to Violet, "look at that spooky house."
As he pointed to it, the front door opened squeakily.

When they went inside, Igor and Ivy dropped a large bucket of green slime on them.

The Wagners ran away.

In the 1950s Ed and Myra Russell were driving home after
a dance lesson. "Jeepers!" said Ed. "Look at this place!"
"I wish we lived here," said Myra. "I'd have room to practice
my cha-cha dance steps."

"Let's look in the windows," she said.

Ed and Myra felt hot breath on their backs. Then something hairy rubbed against their legs.

Ed and Myra left the house in a hurry.

In the 1980s a house saleswoman arrived with the Merry family.
"This house has been empty for as long as I can remember," she said.
"Empty?" the Ghosts asked each other. "*We live here.*"
"It has a certain old-fashioned charm!" said Mrs. Merry.

"Look at this fireplace," said Mr. Merry. "You don't see houses built
like this anymore."

Their two children, Teddy and Alice, slid down the banister.
Spot, their dog, ran up and down the stairs.

"The house is perfect," said the Merrys. "Can we move in tomorrow?"

In the morning a moving van rolled up. "They're not coming to live here!" growled Father Ghost as he dropped large dust balls throughout the house. Mother Ghost draped huge cobwebs all over the doorways.

Igor and Ivy let the bats and snakes loose. "This should scare them," they said.

The Merrys unloaded their furniture and carried it inside.
"Tsk, tsk," said Mrs. Merry. "So dusty. I'll sweep this clean
in minutes."

Mr. Merry opened the attic door and found Egyptian mummies!
"Look at this great old stuff!" he said, chuckling.

That evening the Merrys sipped hot chocolate and sang songs,
while boos and moans were heard in the background.

"They're weird," said Mother Ghost.
"Don't worry," Father Ghost said. "Tonight we'll make them shake in their beds!"

That night the ghosts slammed doors, clanked chains, BOO-OOED, and made a racket.

Mrs. Merry gave earmuffs to everyone, and they all had a good night's sleep.

In the morning the ghosts were tired and cranky.
When Mr. Merry washed his face, a skeleton handed him a towel.
"Thank you," he said, chuckling.

Mrs. Merry opened the oven and hundreds of bats
flew out.

"Oh, my!" she said. "What a dirty oven."

Alice found a huge toad in her bath. She gave it a shampoo
and kissed it!

Teddy found spiders in his breakfast cereal and ate them.

Creepy Cat nipped Spot's tail, making Spot run around the yard in circles.

"How nice," said Mrs. Merry. "Spot is getting some exercise."

That night the full moon shone brightly on the house, and the
Ghosts gathered in the attic to talk.

"It's dreadful," said Mother. "The Merrys seem to *like* living here."

Suddenly a screen door slammed shut. The Ghosts leaned
out of a window to see the Merry family, who seemed to be turning
into...

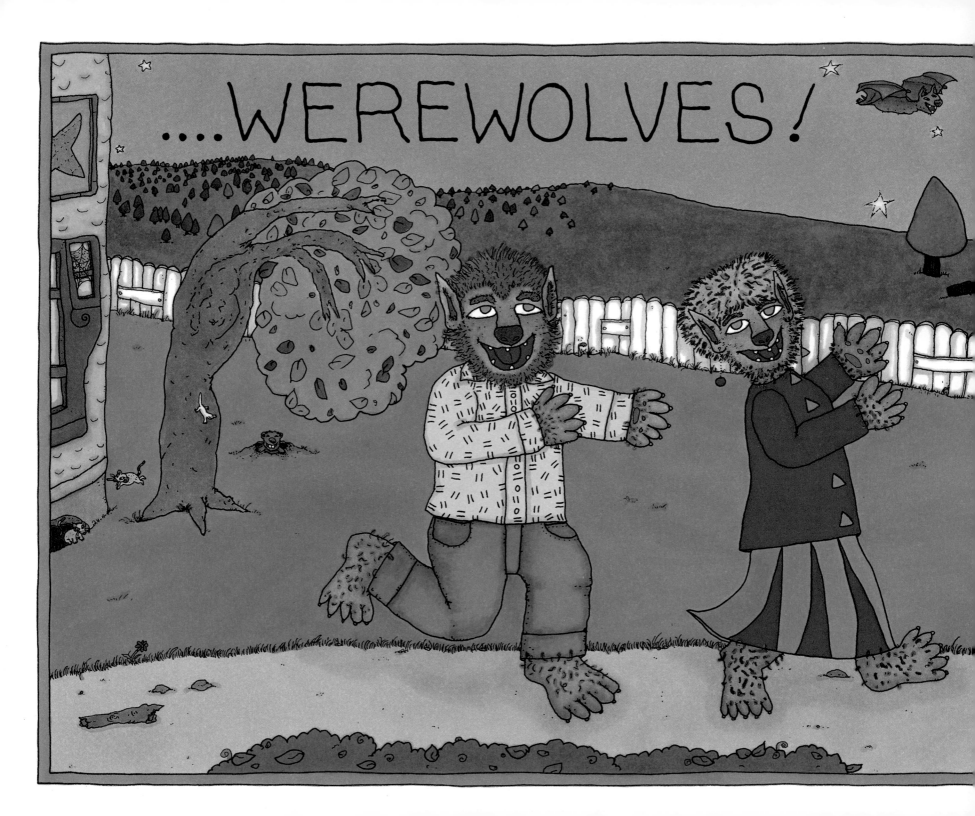

"How nice," said Mother Ghost. "They make the best company!"
"They're not *company*, they're *living* here," moaned Ivy and Igor.
"There's plenty of room for all of us," said Father Ghost.
"Werewolves are always welcome!"
And they all lived happily forever and ever and ever...after!